Learning to Read, Step by Step!

Ready to Read   Preschool–Kindergarten
• big type and easy words • rhyme and rhythm • picture clues
For children who know the alphabet and are eager to begin reading.

Reading with Help   Preschool–Grade 1
• basic vocabulary • short sentences • simple stories
For children who recognize familiar words and sound out new words with help.

Reading on Your Own   Grades 1–3
• engaging characters • easy-to-follow plots • popular topics
For children who are ready to read on their own.

Reading Paragraphs   Grades 2–3
• challenging vocabulary • short paragraphs • exciting stories
For newly independent readers who read simple sentences with confidence.

Ready for Chapters   Grades 2–4
• chapters • longer paragraphs • full-color art
For children who want to take the plunge into chapter books but still like colorful pictures.

STEP INTO READING® is designed to give every child a successful reading experience. The grade levels are only guides. Children can progress through the steps at their own speed, developing confidence in their reading, no matter what their grade.

Remember, a lifetime love of reading starts with a single step!

Copyright © 1999 by Berenstain Enterprises, Inc. All rights reserved under International and Pan-American Copyright Conventions. Published in the United States by Random House Children's Books, a division of Random House, Inc., New York, and simultaneously in Canada by Random House of Canada Limited, Toronto.

www.stepintoreading.com

Educators and librarians, for a variety of teaching tools, visit us at
www.randomhouse.com/teachers

www.berenstainbears.com

Library of Congress Cataloging-in-Publication Data
Berenstain, Stan, 1923– .
The Berenstain Bears go up and down / Stan & Jan Berenstain. p.   cm. — (Step into reading.
A step 1 book) SUMMARY: The Berenstain Bears go up and down on an escalator.
ISBN 0-679-88720-2 (trade) — ISBN 0-679-98720-7 (lib. bdg.)
[1. Bears—Fiction. 2. Escalators—Fiction.] I. Berenstain, Jan, 1923– . II. Title. III. Series:
Step into reading. Step 1 book. PZ7.B4483 Bemkk 2003 [E]—dc21 2002013262

Printed in the United States of America   15 14 13 12 11 10 9 8 7 6

STEP INTO READING, RANDOM HOUSE, and the Random House colophon are registered trademarks of Random House, Inc.

STEP INTO READING®

STEP 1

The Berenstain Bears

GO UP AND DOWN

A Math Reader

The Berenstains

Random House New York

One bear going up.

Two bears coming down.

Three bears going up.

Four bears coming down.

One bear coming
down the UP.

Two bears going
up the DOWN.

Three bears coming
down the UP.

Four bears going
up the DOWN.

Ten bears up—

UP

all piled up.

Ten bears down—

all piled up.

Ten bears up.

Ten bears down.

"Let's do it again!"

say both groups of ten.

"STOP! STOP!"

says a cop.

Twenty bears
all lined up.